THE LITTLE ENGINE THAT COULD

This book is dedicated to my mother, Elizabeth Long,
who knows something of climbing mountains —L. L.

She would start with a soft whisper . . . I think I can, I think I can, I think I can. Slowly her voice would grow . . . I think I can, I think I can, I think I can. Until finally with a resolute confidence, she'd read, . . . I think I can, I think I can, I think I can.

Even today as an adult, a father myself, I can still hear my mother's voice and that familiar cadence as she would read those powerful words to me. I can see the rocking chair we would sit in together in my bedroom, and I still feel the warmth of those moments.

Though multitudes of people have read *The Little Engine That Could,* spanning many generations, when I was a young boy it seemed to have been written and created only for me. It was my book, it was my story and it was my message.

I loved the spunk of Little Blue and her willing determination has inspired and actually sustained me in some pretty harrying instances throughout my life.

I'm comforted by the knowledge that my grandma read *The Little Engine That Could* over and over to my mother all the way back in the 1940s when she was a little girl. My mother then read it to me time and time again when I was little. I have now read it to my little boys over and over again. And one day, perhaps, my two sons will read *The Little Engine That Could* again and again to their own children . . . my grandkids.

THE LITTLE ENGINE THAT COULD

retold by
Watty Piper

with new art by
Loren Long

PHILOMEL BOOKS   *in association with* GROSSET & DUNLAP

Chug, chug, chug. Puff, puff, puff. Ding-dong, ding-dong. The little train rumbled over the tracks. She was a happy little train for she had such a jolly load to carry. Her cars were filled full of good things for boys and girls.

There were toy animals—giraffes with long necks, Teddy
bears with almost no necks at all, and even a baby elephant. Then
there were dolls—dolls with blue eyes and yellow curls, dolls with
brown eyes and brown bobbed heads, and the funniest little toy
clown you ever saw.

And there were cars full of toy engines, airplanes, tops, jack-knives, picture puzzles, books, and every kind of thing boys or girls could want.

But that was not all. Some of the cars were filled with all sorts of good things for boys and girls to eat—big golden oranges, red-cheeked apples, bottles of creamy milk for their breakfasts, fresh spinach for their dinners, peppermint drops, and lollypops for after-meal treats.

The little train was carrying all these wonderful things to the good little boys and girls on the other side of the mountain.
She puffed along merrily.

Then all of a sudden she stopped with a jerk. She simply
could not go another inch. She tried and she tried, but her wheels
would not turn.

What were all those good little boys and girls on the other side of the mountain going to do without the wonderful toys to play with and the good food to eat?

"Here comes a shiny new engine," said the funny little clown
who jumped out of the train. "Let us ask him to help us."
So all the dolls and toys cried out together:
"Please, Shiny New Engine, won't you please pull our train

over the mountain? Our engine has broken down, and the boys and girls on the other side won't have any toys to play with or good food to eat unless you help us."

But the Shiny New Engine snorted: "I pull you? I am a
Passenger Engine. I have just carried a fine big train over the
mountain, with more cars than you ever dreamed of. My train
had sleeping cars, with comfortable berths; a dining-car where

waiters bring whatever hungry people want to eat; and parlor cars
in which people sit in soft arm-chairs and look out of big plate-
glass windows.

"I pull the likes of you? Indeed not!"

And off he steamed to the roundhouse, where engines live when they are not busy.

How sad the little train and all the dolls and toys felt!

Then the little clown called out, "The Passenger Engine is not the only one in the world. Here is another engine coming, a great big strong one. Let us ask him to help us."

The little toy clown waved his flag and the big strong engine came to a stop.

"Please, oh, please, Big Engine," cried all the dolls and toys together. "Won't you please pull our train over the mountain? Our engine has broken down, and the good little boys and girls on the other side won't have any toys to play with or good food to eat unless you help us."

But the Big Strong Engine bellowed: "I am a Freight Engine. I have just pulled a big train loaded with big machines over the mountain. These machines print books and newspapers for grown-ups to read. I am a very important engine indeed. I won't pull the likes of you!"

And the Freight Engine puffed off indignantly to the roundhouse.

The little train and all the dolls and toys were very sad.

"Cheer up," cried the little toy clown. "The Freight Engine is not the only one in the world. Here comes another. He looks very old and tired, but our train is so little, perhaps he can help us."

So the little toy clown waved his flag and the dingy, rusty old engine stopped.

"Please, Kind Engine," cried all the dolls and toys together.

"Won't you please pull our train over the mountain? Our engine has broken down, and the boys and girls on the other side won't have any toys to play with or good food to eat unless you help us."

But the Rusty Old Engine sighed: "I am so tired. I must rest my weary wheels. I cannot pull even so little a train as yours over the mountain. I can not. I can not. I can not."

And off he rumbled to the roundhouse chugging, "I can not. I can not. I can not."

Then indeed the little train was very, very sad, and the dolls

and toys were ready to cry.

But the little clown called out, "Here is another engine coming,
a little blue engine, a very little one, maybe she will help us."

The very little engine came chug, chugging merrily along.
When she saw the toy clown's flag, she stopped quickly.

"What is the matter, my friends?" she asked kindly.

"Oh, Little Blue Engine," cried the dolls and toys. "Will you pull us over the mountain? Our engine has broken down and the

good boys and girls on the other side won't have any toys to play
with or good food to eat, unless you help us. Please, please, help
us, Little Blue Engine."

"I'm not very big," said the Little Blue Engine. "They use me only for switching trains in the yard. I have never been over the mountain."

"But we must get over the mountain before the children awake," said all the dolls and the toys.

The very little engine looked up and saw the tears in the dolls' eyes. And she thought of the good little boys and girls on the other side of the mountain who would not have any toys or good food unless she helped.

Then she said, "I think I can. I think I can. I think I can." And she hitched herself to the little train.

She tugged and pulled and pulled and tugged and slowly, slowly, slowly they started off.

The toy clown jumped aboard and all the dolls and the toy animals began to smile and cheer.

Puff, puff, chug, chug, went the Little Blue Engine. "I think
I can—I think I can—I think I can—I think I can—I think I
can—I think I can—I think I can—I think I can—I think I can."

Up, up, up. Faster and faster and faster and faster the little engine climbed,

until at last they reached the top of the mountain.

Down in the valley lay the city.

"Hurray, hurray," cried the funny little clown and all the dolls and toys.

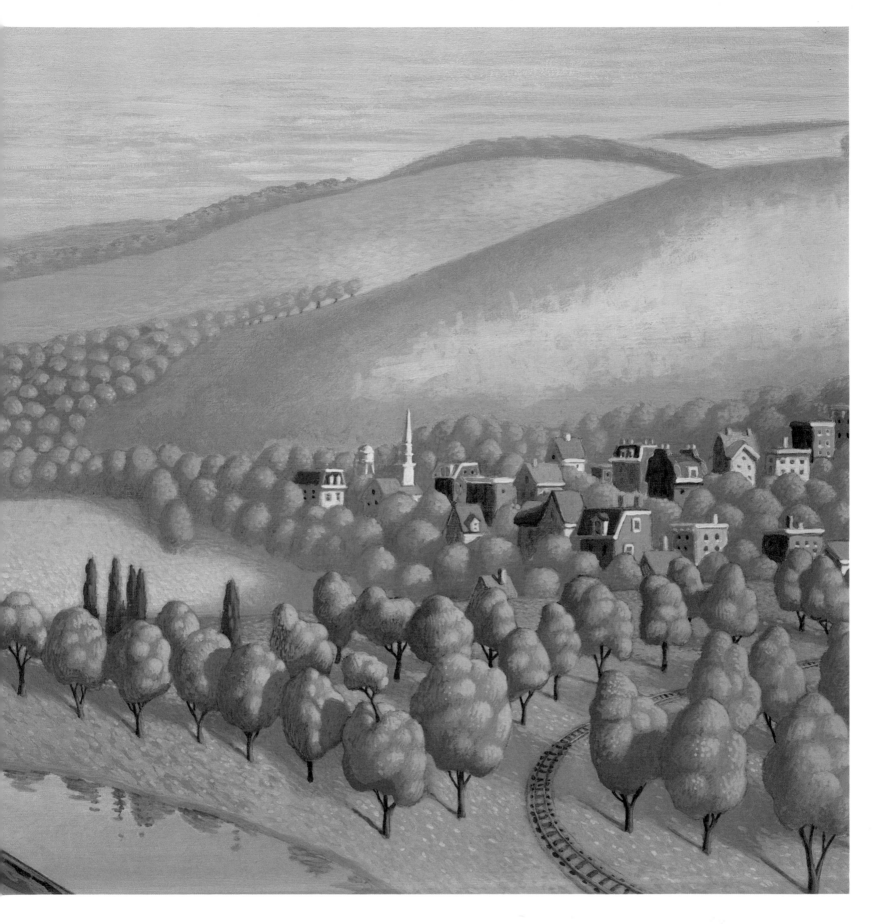

"The good little boys and girls in the city will be happy because you helped us, kind, Little Blue Engine."

And the Little Blue Engine smiled and seemed to say as she puffed steadily down the mountain, "I thought I could. I thought I could. I thought I could. I thought I could. I thought I could. I thought I could."

Special thanks to Patti Gauch for sharing her wisdom and enthusiasm, to Semadar Megged for her dedication and for being herself, to Doug Whiteman for his confidence in me, and to Nicholas Callaway for his vision. —L.L.

PATRICIA LEE GAUCH, EDITOR

Copyright © 2005 Penguin Group (USA) Inc.
The Little Engine That Could, *I Think I Can* and all related titles, logos, and characters are trademarks of Penguin Group (USA) Inc.

Illustrations by Loren Long.

PHILOMEL BOOKS
in association with GROSSET & DUNLAP
Divisions of Penguin Young Readers Group.   Published by The Penguin Group.
Penguin Group (USA) Inc., 375 Hudson Street, New York, NY 10014, U.S.A.
Penguin Group (Canada), 10 Alcorn Avenue, Toronto, Ontario, Canada M4V 3B2 (a division of Pearson Penguin Canada Inc.)
Penguin Books Ltd, 80 Strand, London WC2R 0RL, England.
Penguin Ireland, 25 St. Stephen's Green, Dublin 2, Ireland (a division of Penguin Books Ltd.)
Penguin Group (Australia), 250 Camberwell Road, Camberwell, Victoria 3124, Australia (a division of Pearson Australia Group Pty Ltd).
Penguin Books India Pvt Ltd, 11 Community Centre, Panchsheel Park, New Delhi - 110 017, India.
Penguin Group (NZ), Cnr Airborne and Rosedale Roads, Albany, Auckland 1310, New Zealand (a division of Pearson New Zealand Ltd).
Penguin Books (South Africa) (Pty) Ltd, 24 Sturdee Avenue, Rosebank, Johannesburg 2196, South Africa.
Penguin Books Ltd, Registered Offices: 80 Strand, London WC2R 0RL, England.

Design by Semadar Megged.   Text set in 20-point Pastonchi.   The illustrations are rendered in acrylic.

Library of Congress Cataloging-in-Publication Data
Piper, Watty, pseud.   The little engine that could / retold by Watty Piper ; with new art by Loren Long. p. cm.
Summary: Although she is not very big, the Little Blue Engine agrees to try to pull a stranded train full of toys over the mountain.
[1. Railroads—Trains—Fiction. 2. Toys—Fiction.] I. Long, Loren, ill. II. Title. PZ7.P64Li 2005 [E]—dc22 2004030496

ISBN 0-399-24467-0
3 5 7 9 10 8 6 4 2

The Little Engine That Could is one of the most popular and famous children's books of all time. Over the years, it has sold many millions of copies. This newly illustrated edition is based on "The Complete, Original Edition," retold by Watty Piper and illustrated by George and Doris Hauman, originally published by Platt and Munk, now part of the Penguin Young Readers Group. Over the years, its title and its refrain of "I think I can" have become a permanent part of the American vernacular.

Loren Long graduated with a BA in Graphic Design/Art Studio from the University of Kentucky, and pursued graduate-level studies at the American Academy of Art in Chicago. He has received numerous accolades for his fluid WPA painting style, including two gold medals from the Society of Illustrators in New York, and the prestigious Golden Kite Award.

Long is the illustrator of many celebrated picture books for children, including Madonna's *Mr. Peabody's Apples, The Day the Animals Came* by Frances Ward Weller, and *I Dream of Trains* by Angela Johnson.

Loren Long lives in a Cincinnati suburb with his wife and two sons.

To learn more about the artist and his work, visit his website at www.lorenlong.com